One to Ten
and
Back Again

For

1. Millie
   2. Rosie   6. Ina
   3. Isabel   7. Ettie
    4. Gabriel   8. Mairi
5. Jim   9. Carina
     10. Thomas

From Nick and Sue

PUFFIN BOOKS
UK | USA | Canada | Ireland | Australia | India | New Zealand | South Africa
Puffin Books is part of the Penguin Random House group of companies
whose addresses can be found at global.penguinrandomhouse.com.
www.penguin.co.uk   www.puffin.co.uk   www.ladybird.co.uk

Penguin
Random House
UK

First published 2004
This edition published 2014
002

Text and illustrations copyright © Sue Heap and Nick Sharratt, 2004
The moral right of the authors has been asserted

Printed in China

The authorized representative in the EEA is Penguin Random House Ireland,
Morrison Chambers, 32 Nassau Street, Dublin D02 YH68

A CIP catalogue record for this book is available from the British Library
ISBN: 978–0–723–29649–2

All correspondence to:
Puffin Books, Penguin Random House Children's
One Embassy Gardens, 8 Viaduct Gardens, London SW11 7BW

One to Ten and Back Again

Sue Heap and Nick Sharratt

PUFFIN

One boy called Nick,

One girl called Sue,

Two woolly gloves,

Two shiny shoes.

Three round buttons,

Four bright bows,

Five pink pigs,

Six sheep in a row.

Seven bobbing boats,

Eight fish in the sea,

Nine chocolate biscuits

and ten cakes for tea.

Ten oranges,

Nine lemons,

Eight crayons,

Seven pens,

Six butterflies,

Five bumble bees,

Four ducks

and three red hens.

Two elephants,

Two crocodiles,

One Sue, one Nick,

Best friends!

One yellow moon,

that's how the story ends!

a hundred stars,

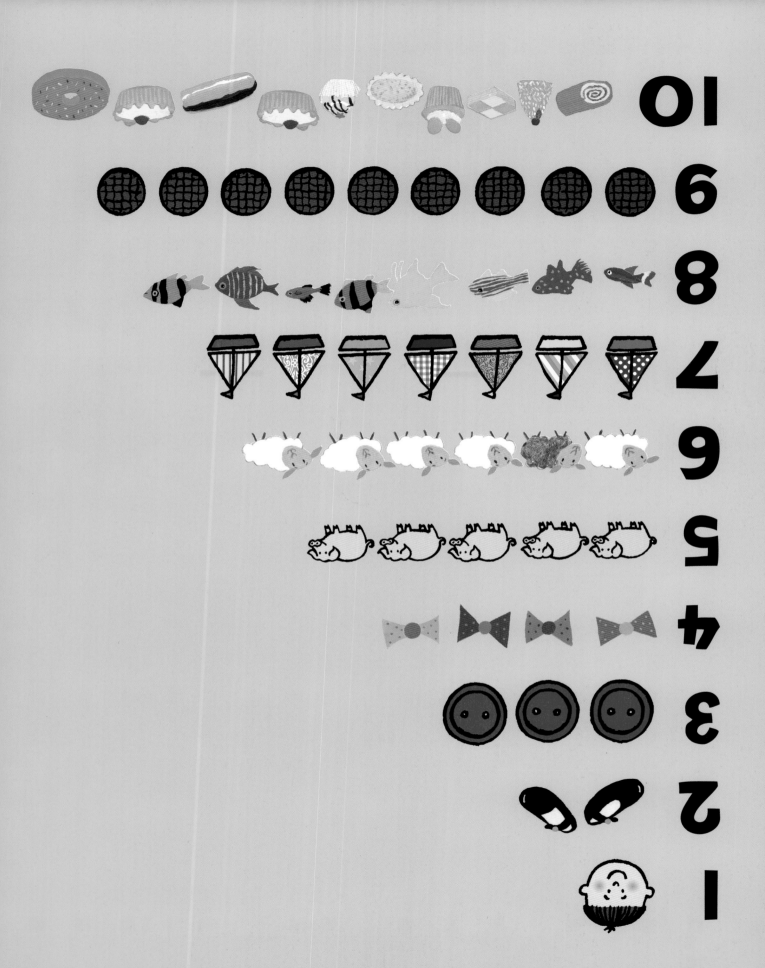

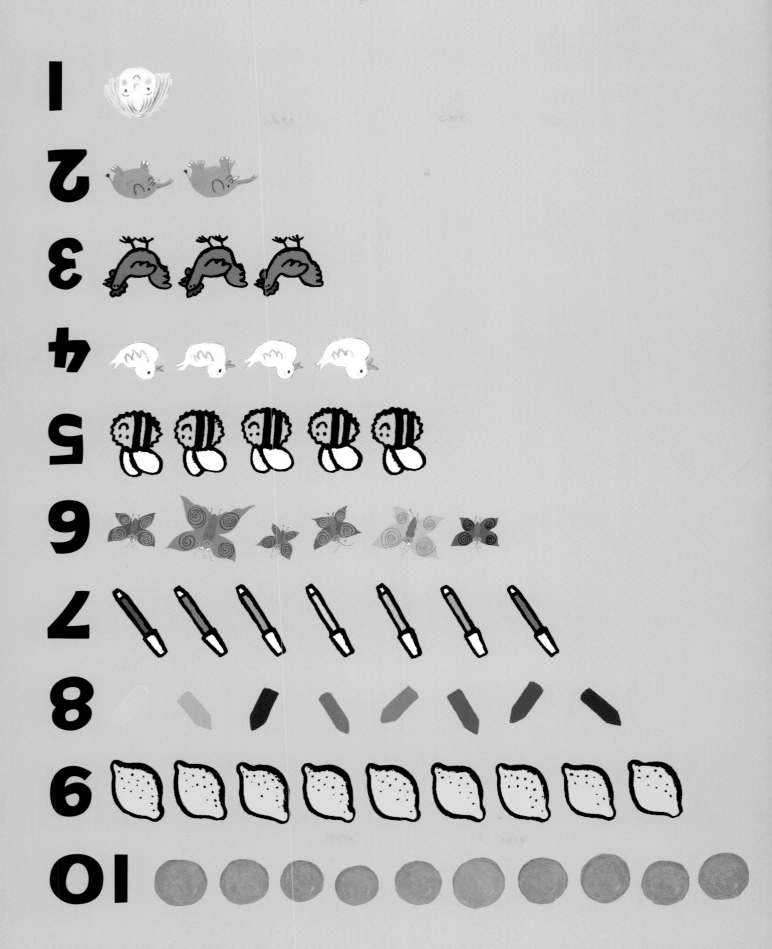

Goodbye, Nick!
Goodbye, Sue!

IMAGINE THAT

Licensed exclusively to Imagine That Publishing Ltd
Tide Mill Way, Woodbridge, Suffolk, IP12 1AP, UK
www.imaginethat.com
Copyright © 2020 Imagine That Group Ltd
All rights reserved
2 4 6 8 9 7 5 3
Manufactured in China

Written by Susie Linn
Illustrated by Gabi Murphy

ISBN 978-1-78958-266-6

A catalogue record for this book is available from the British Library

Can you count the stars?

Written by Susie Linn

Illustrated by Gabi Murphy

Can you count the stars that nightly twinkle in the bedtime sky?

Spot them shining, glowing brightly,
time to wave the day goodbye.

Can you count your clothes that quickly fall in heaps upon the floor?

All the things that Mummy swiftly places back inside the drawer.

Can you count the bubbles popping,
one by one in steamy air?

Seven rubber ducks are bobbing, bathtime fun for little bear!

Can you count as you are brushing
tiny teeth to keep them strong?

Up and down ten times, no rushing!
Make them shine, it won't take long!

Can you count your robe so cosy,
PJs, slippers – one and two?

Snuggle up, with cheeks so rosy,
night clothes red and white and blue.

Can you count as you are kissing everyone around the house?

Mummy, brother, who is missing?
'Goodnight squirrel, goodnight mouse!'

Can you count the books that nestle neatly on your bedroom shelf?

Daddy reads two while you settle,
then he chooses one himself.

Can you count the owls a-listening
to each bedtime tale with you?

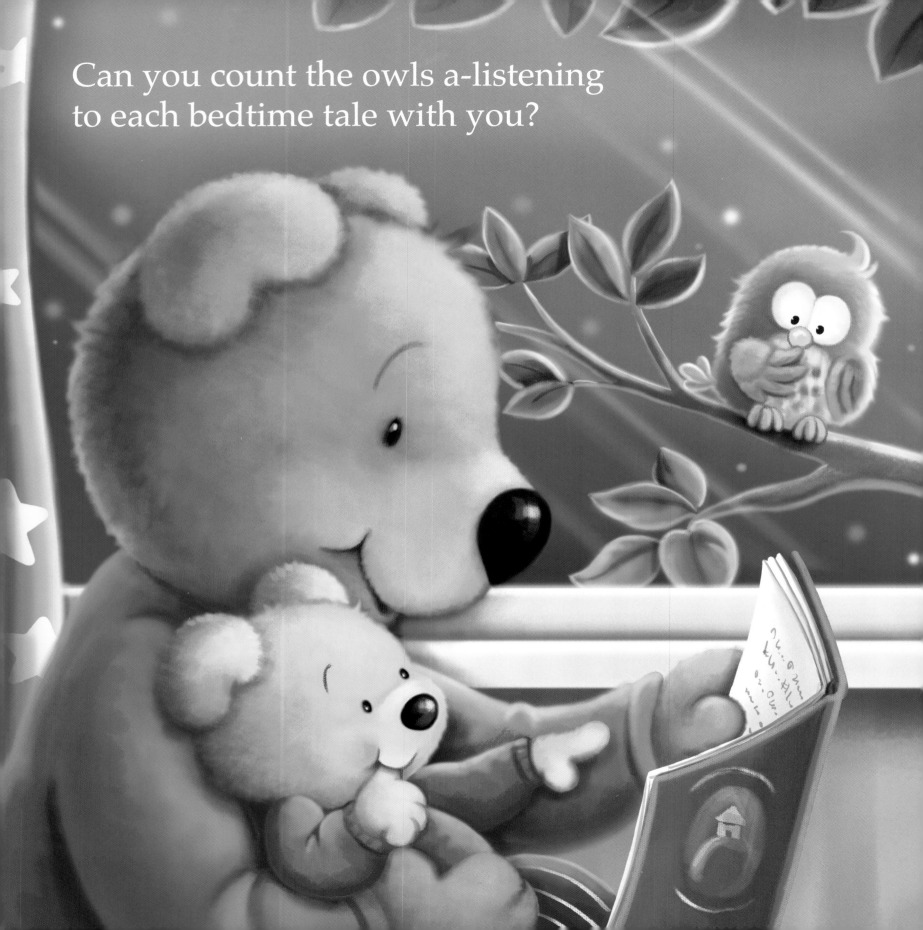

In the moonlight, white and glistening,
little owls, 'twit-twoo, twit-twoo!'

Can you count the toys that huddle,
all around you in your bed?

Time to give each one a cuddle,
hug them all, then rest your head.

Can you count, while you are dozing,
three things that you did today?

Happy thoughts – your eyes are closing,
fun with friends who came to play.

Can you count the shapes that turning,
gently light your bedroom wall?

Night-light creatures watching, guarding,
as deeper into sleep you fall.

Can you count the moon so brightly,
shining on you, little bear?

While you sleep, your eyes closed tightly,
dream tonight without a care.